W9-CND-426

A Note to Parents and Caregivers:

*Read-it!* Readers are for children who are just starting on the amazing road to reading. These beautiful books support both the acquisition of reading skills and the love of books.

The PURPLE LEVEL presents basic topics and objects using high frequency words and simple language patterns.

The RED LEVEL presents familiar topics using common words and repeating sentence patterns.

The BLUE LEVEL presents new ideas using a larger vocabulary and varied sentence structure.

The YELLOW LEVEL presents more challenging ideas, a broad vocabulary, and wide variety in sentence structure.

The GREEN LEVEL presents more complex ideas, an extended vocabulary range, and expanded language structures.

The ORANGE LEVEL presents a wide range of ideas and concepts using challenging vocabulary and complex language structures.

When sharing a book with your child, read in short stretches, pausing often to talk about the pictures. Have your child turn the pages and point to the pictures and familiar words. And be sure to reread favorite stories or parts of stories.

There is no right or wrong way to share books with children. Find time to read with your child, and pass on the legacy of literacy.

Adria F. Klein, Ph.D.
Professor Emeritus
California State University
San Bernardino, California

Editor: Patricia Stockland
Page production: Melissa Kes/JoAnne Nelson/Tracy Davies
Art Director: Keith Griffin
Managing Editor: Catherine Neitge
The illustrations in this book were rendered in acrylic.

Picture Window Books
5115 Excelsior Boulevard
Suite 232
Minneapolis, MN 55416
877-845-8392
www.picturewindowbooks.com

Printed in the United States of America.

**Library of Congress Cataloging-in-Publication Data**
Blair, Eric.
Pecos Bill / by Eric Blair ; illustrated by Micah Chambers-Goldberg.
p. cm. — (Read-it! readers: tall tales)
Summary: Relates some of the legends of Pecos Bill, a cowboy who was raised by wild
animals, once roped a whole herd of cattle at once, and invented Texas chili.
ISBN 1-4048-0977-5 (hardcover)
1. Pecos Bill (Legendary character)—Legends. [1. Pecos Bill (Legendary character)—
Legends. 2. Folklore—United States. 3. Tall tales.] I. Chambers-Goldberg, Micah, ill.
II. Title. III. Read-it! readers tall tales.
PZ8.1.B5824Pe 2004
398.2'0973'02—dc22                                              2004018437

# Pecos Bill

## By Eric Blair
## Illustrated by Micah Chambers-Goldberg

Special thanks to our advisers for their expertise:

Adria F. Klein, Ph.D.
Professor Emeritus, California State University
San Bernardino, California

Susan Kesselring, M.A.
Literacy Educator
Rosemount-Apple Valley-Eagan (Minnesota) School District

PICTURE WINDOW BOOKS
Minneapolis, Minnesota

Pecos Bill was the youngest of eighteen children.

When Bill was a baby, his family decided to move to the Wild West.

When the covered wagon crossed the Pecos River, baby Bill fell out into the water. His brothers, sisters, Mom, and Dad didn't notice until it was too late to save him.

Bill floated down the river until a mother coyote grabbed him from the water.

The mother coyote adopted Bill. She raised him like he was one of her pups.

Bill grew up in the wild.

He became friends with the
rattlesnakes and mountain lions.

After a while, Bill thought he was a coyote. One day, a cowboy found Bill sleeping in the brush.

The cowboy taught Bill reading, riding, and arithmetic.

READIN

RIDIN

AND

ARITH

Pecos Bill became a famous cowboy. He rode a horse no one else could ride. Its name was Widow-Maker.

Bill became an expert at breaking wild horses. He could ride and rope better than any man alive.

Once, Pecos Bill lassoed a whole herd of Longhorn cattle, but not one at a time. He roped the whole herd at once!

Another time, Pecos Bill rode a
mountain lion into town just to
see the looks on people's faces.

A few years later, Pecos Bill roped a twister to save that same town. Afterwards, for fun, he rode the twister home.

19

Pecos Bill also loved to sing. He wrote a lullaby to relax the cattle.

They never wandered off at night because they were asleep.

Pecos Bill loved to swim, too. That's how he met the love of his life.

One day, Bill was swimming in the river.

Suddenly, Slue-Foot Sue rode by on a huge catfish. Sue was the girl of Bill's dreams.

Sue agreed to marry Bill, but only if he let her ride his horse, Widow-Maker.

No one but Bill had ever ridden
Widow-Maker and lived.

When Sue tried to ride Widow-Maker, the horse bucked her all the way into the sky, beyond the clouds, and to the moon.

Sue landed right back
on Widow-Maker.

The horse was so surprised that it never bucked her off again.

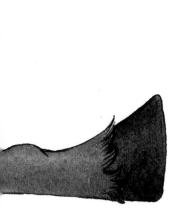

Pecos Bill and Slue-Foot Sue were married that very same day. Together, they rode catfish, roped twisters, and lived happily ever after.

# More *Read-it!* Readers

Bright pictures and fun stories help you practice your reading skills. Look for more books at your level.

## TALL TALES
*Annie Oakley, Sharp Shooter* by Eric Blair
*John Henry* by Christianne C. Jones
*Johnny Appleseed* by Eric Blair
*The Legend of Daniel Boone* by Eric Blair
*Paul Bunyan* by Eric Blair
*Pecos Bill* by Eric Blair

Looking for a specific title or level? A complete list of *Read-it!* Readers is available on our Web site: *www.picturewindowbooks.com*